Apples for All

Written by
Qi Zhi

Illustrated by
Cheng Yue

CARDINAL
MEDIA

Ben the monkey sat up in a tree eating apples.

Then Ben picked some apples and climbed over a fence to head home.

On his way, Ben met
Frederick the fawn and
Peppermint the pony.

Ben shared some apples with them.
"Yum!" they said. "We wish we could
climb over the fence to get some apples."

Ben had an idea. "Let's plant a tree here.
Then there will be apples for all!"

He dug a hole and buried an apple core in the soil.

He showed Peppermint
how to water it every day.

He showed Frederick how
the tree was starting to grow.

Up, up, the young tree grew as tall as Frederick.

Then it grew as tall
as Peppermint.

Frederick and Peppermint watered the young tree together.

The tree grew taller and taller. It was so tall that only Ben could reach its top.

The big tree flowered and was
filled with many red apples.

They invited their friends
to an apple party.

Ben climbed up the tree, picked the apples, and threw them to his friends.

Ben shook the branches, and more apples dropped to the ground.

Everyone enjoyed the apples. They were so happy. There were apples for all.

Apples For All

When a monkey
learns his friends can't
reach an apple tree,
his clever idea leads
to apples for all.

CARDINAL
MEDIA

Cardinal Media, LLC.
8501 West Higgins Road, Suite 790
Chicago, Illinois 60631
www.cardinalmediakids.com

CANADIAN RETAIL: $5.99

ISBN 978-1-64074-034-1

9 781640 740341

Printed in China